StarFriends

MIRROR MAGIC

ucy Fleming, 20

5-786-7

to be ide

been

To any of my readers who believe in
magic as much as I do... – LC

To Kim – LF

STRIPES PUBLISHING
An imprint of the Little Tiger Group
1 The Coda Centre, 189 Munster Road,
London SW6 6AW

A paperback original
First published in Great Britain in 2017

Text copyright © Linda Chapman, 2017
Illustrations copy███████████████████17

A CIP catalogue record for this book is available from
the British Library.

Printed and bound in the UK.

2 4 6 8 10 9 7 5 3 1

Star Friends
Mirror Magic

Linda Chapman
ILLUSTRATED BY LUCY FLEMING

In the Star World

The sky was a velvet-black and everything
glittered with stardust – the animals, the trees,
the meadows, the rivers and the mountains.
They all shone. It was a special night and a
large crowd of animals was gathered around
a waterfall made of stars that tumbled into a
bottomless pool. The air hummed with chatter
as they waited for the event to start.

At the front of the crowd there were eight
young animals – a fox, an otter, a badger, a
wildcat, a deer, a squirrel, a sparrowhawk and

a dormouse. The squirrel scampered over to the fox and stood up on his back legs, his shimmering tail curling like a comma behind him. "It's almost time for us to travel to the human world, Bracken."

"I can't wait!" the fox said, spinning round with excitement, his indigo eyes shining. "It's going to be such an adventure."

The deer's ears flickered anxiously. "Aren't you two nervous? I am."

The wildcat rolled her eyes. "What a surprise! You're scared of everything, Willow. Why don't you just stay at home?"

Bracken gave her a look of dislike and touched the deer's nose with his. "Don't listen to her. You're brave, Willow, I know you are. And besides, we'll be together — at least to start with. You'll be all right."

Willow, the deer, nuzzled him gratefully.

A large owl with silvery wings swooped silently into the clearing. As he perched on a branch beside the waterfall, the crowd of animals fell silent. This was the moment they had been waiting for.

"Welcome, my friends," Hunter the owl called out. "Once again, the time has come for us to send a group of young Star Animals to the human world. Each of these animals will have the task of finding a Star Friend – a child who believes in magic."

Hunter looked at the animals around him and continued speaking. "These new Star Friends will be taught how to use the magic that flows between our world and the human world to do good deeds, bringing happiness and peace. As you know, usually only two or three Star Animals travel to the human world together but today eight will be making the journey." An excited murmur rose from the crowd. The owl held up his wing.

"We are sending more animals this time because the human world is in trouble. Fewer humans believe in magic, which means fewer people are using Star Magic to do good, and the current of magic that flows between our world and the human world is growing weak. But there's something even more worrying." The owl looked solemn. "We sense someone in the human world is using dark magic to hurt people and cause unhappiness. If this is so, it must not continue."

He turned to the young animals at the front of the crowd. "The eight of you will be sent to the place where we believe dark magic is being used – where the Star Magic is weakest. You must find out what is going on and stop it. But, first, you each need to find a human child to be your Star Friend. A child who is kind-hearted enough to use magic for good and brave enough to defeat someone using dark magic. When you meet a child you think could be a Star Friend, speak to them with your thoughts. If they are open to magic, they will hear you."

"What will happen to us when we're in the human world, Hunter?" said the squirrel, jumping on to Bracken's back. "Will we still sparkle and shine like we do now?" He waved his tail, making every hair glitter.

The owl shook his head. "No, Juniper. You will look like a normal animal, apart from your indigo eyes. However, unlike a normal animal, you will be able to appear and disappear."

"Will we all find Star Friends in the same place?" asked the otter.

"I do not think so," Hunter replied. "It is rare to find children who truly believe in magic these days and there are unlikely to be eight such children in the same place. If you do not find a Star Friend when you arrive, then travel on. Choose wisely. Once you have found a Star Friend, you will stay with them for their whole lives, guiding and helping them and fighting dark magic."

The wildcat stood up. "When do we leave?"

"As soon as you wish, Sorrel," said the owl. "Simply step under the stream of stars in the waterfall."

"I'm going first!" said Bracken. "Goodbye, everyone!" He darted past Sorrel, who hissed at him in anger. With an excited bark, he leaped into the waterfall and vanished in a cloud of sparkles.

"Rude creature!" the wildcat spat. She gave a haughty flick of her tail, walked to the waterfall and stepped carefully into the stars, vanishing. The animals' voices rose with excitement.

One by one the other young animals followed until, last of all, the dormouse jumped through the waterfall and disappeared.

The owl turned to the crowd. "Let us hope our young friends succeed in finding Star Friends and defeating those who use magic for evil purposes," he said. "I fear that the human world needs Star Animals now more than ever."

He flapped his wings and soared away into the dark sky.

CHAPTER ONE

Mountain gorilla, orangutan, Galapagos penguin…

Maia Greene blew her dark blond fringe out of her eyes and turned the pages of the book on endangered animals. It was so hard to choose just one.

"Hurry up now, everyone," called Miss Harris. "There's just five minutes until break time. I want you to have decided on your project by then."

Maia turned the pages more quickly.

Maybe a penguin? They always made her giggle with their funny waddling walk. Or an African wild dog? She loved dogs. Or a wolf? She paused at a photograph of a grey wolf. Her Granny Anne had loved wolves and had kept lots of wolf ornaments and paintings in her cottage. Maia's heart twisted in her chest. Granny Anne had died last month and Maia still missed her a lot. No, wolves would make her feel too sad.

"I can't believe you still haven't decided," said Ionie, who sat next to her. "I've already done a whole page of notes on my animal." She flicked her strawberry blond ponytail over her shoulder and showed Maia a page of neat writing with headings underlined with a ruler.

"I have decided," said Maia defensively. "I'm going to do my project on … on … orangutans." She picked an animal at random just to shut Ionie up. Ever since they had been put on the same table at the start of term, Ionie had been driving her crazy. It was bad enough that Sita and Lottie, her best friends, were in the other Year Six class, but having to sit next to Ionie seemed very unfair. Ionie was clever and she loved pointing out any mistakes Maia made.

"Orangutans? Really?" Ionie sighed. "Can't you be more imaginative than that? There are at least four other people doing orangutans."

"So what amazing, unusual animal have you decided to do your project on?" Maia asked.

"A pronghorn," Ionie answered. "Do you even know what a pronghorn is?"

Maia hadn't heard of a pronghorn. Still, she didn't want to admit that to Ionie so she hazarded a guess. "Is it some kind of deer?"

She saw Ionie's face fall slightly and knew she must have got it right.

"Kind of," Ionie admitted. "It's a bit like a deer and a bit like a goat and a bit like an antelope, although actually it's a totally unique animal. Anyway, why don't I find you something that's more interesting than orangutans." She opened the book on her section of the desk. "Maybe you could do your project on a saola or a pangolin – they were my reserve choices—"

"OK, everyone. It's break time!" Miss Harris called.

Maia jumped up before she had to admit to Ionie that she didn't know what either of those animals were. She tidied her books away and headed outside.

Lottie and Sita were waiting for her by the coat hooks – Lottie, small and skinny, her curly black hair clipped back with a pink butterfly slide, and Sita, tall and graceful, with her shiny dark brown hair in a thick plait.

"Escape at last!" Maia said, immediately feeling better at the sight of them.

"Your lesson was that bad?" said Sita sympathetically.

"*Any* lesson sitting next to Ionie is bad," said Maia.

Sita's eyes widened in warning. Glancing back, Maia saw that Ionie had followed her to the classroom doorway with an open book about endangered animals in her hands.

"Well, that's the last time I bother trying to help *you* with a project, Maia Greene!" she snapped and she marched back inside.

Maia felt a rush of guilt. She didn't like upsetting people – even people as irritating as Ionie.

"Whoops," Lottie muttered.

"Wait here." Maia hurried back into the classroom. Ionie was standing by their table. "Ionie, I'm sorry…"

"Forget it," Ionie said abruptly, picking up a book. "It's not as if I care what you and your silly little gang think."

Maia bit her bottom lip, not knowing what to say.

Ionie turned her back. "I'm going to read," she said. "Go away."

Maia sighed and went back to the coat hooks. "Well, that was awkward," she told the others.

"It's her own fault," said Lottie loyally.

"She shouldn't be so annoying. It must be horrible having to sit with her." She tucked her arm in Maia's. "Come on, get your coat and let's go outside."

"So, what have you been doing this morning?" Sita asked Maia as they went into the playground. The October sun was shining but a cold breeze was making fallen leaves skitter across the ground.

"Miss Harris was telling us all about endangered animals," said Maia, zipping up her coat and burying her hands in her pockets. "She told us how many species are dying out and about how people need to do more to help…" An idea suddenly popped into her head. "You know it's the Harvest Show in the village hall next weekend? Well, why don't we ask if we can run a cake stall to raise money for endangered animals? We'll have all half-term to prepare for it and do some baking."

"Oh yes, let's!" said Sita.

"Great idea! We could bake loads of different cakes," said Lottie. "My dad's helping to organize the show. I'll ask him if he can sort out a table for us."

Maia beamed. "Perfect. If you come round to mine tomorrow morning we can choose which cakes we're going to bake and practise baking them."

"OK, but it'll have to be before my gymnastics at eleven thirty," said Lottie. "It's a cool idea, Maia."

Maia grinned. It really was.

Maia's mum was waiting for her in the car after school. She could see her eighteen-month-old brother, Alfie, strapped into his car seat. He gave Maia a toy car as she opened the back door.

"Ook! Car!" he said proudly.

Maia grinned. "Yes, car," she said. She was glad

to get out of the cold and into the warm car.

"Half-term starts now!" her mum said, smiling at her and starting the engine. "A whole week off. I bet that feels good."

"It does," Maia said. "No more Ionie!"

Ionie had spent half the afternoon ignoring Maia and the other half of it pointing out spelling mistakes in her write-up of a science experiment on cress that they had been doing. Maia's guilt over upsetting her that morning had quickly faded.

Her mum tutted. "Oh, Maia, that's not very nice. You used to be good friends."

"In Reception and Year One, before she started being so annoying," Maia said.

It was true that she and Ionie had got on when they started school. Ionie was six months older than Maia and she'd always had really good ideas for games – fun things, not just playing tag or hide-and-seek like everyone else, but pretending to be dolphins or imagining they had unicorns of their own. But then Ionie had started to get really bossy and so Maia had made friends with Lottie and Sita instead.

"Can't you be friends again?" said her mum. "I was talking to Ionie's mum and she says Ionie's lonely."

Maia didn't believe it. "She doesn't act like she's lonely and wants to be friends with people. If we're all talking together, she just goes off and reads a book, and if she has to join in, she tells everyone their ideas are rubbish and hers are the best."

"It might be because she's an only child," Mrs Greene said. "I was one so I know what it's like. It's sometimes difficult to know how to fit in. She might secretly want to make friends with you all."

"Mmm," said Maia disbelievingly. She changed the subject. "Are we going straight home?"

"No. We're going to Granny Anne's house

to collect some stuff for the charity shop. Dad's meeting us there, and then he'll go on and pick up Clio after netball practice."

"Dactor!" shouted Alfie, pointing at a tractor out of the window.

"Yes, tractor! And look, there's a digger, too!" said Maia, pointing things out as her mum drove on through the twisty streets of Westcombe.

Maia had lived in Westcombe all her life – it was a large village on the North Devon coast and Maia loved it. On sunny days she and her mum, dad, Alfie and older sister Clio would go to the shingle beach and have picnics. On stormy, wintry days they would wrap up in raincoats and go for blustery walks, stopping for a hot chocolate at the Copper Kettle tearoom afterwards.

Her mum drove across the main road on to a small bumpy lane that led towards the beach. There were a few houses at the top of the lane and halfway down was Granny Anne's white stone cottage with its thatched roof and small windows.

The car pulled up outside. Maia shivered. The curtains had been pulled across the windows ever since Granny Anne had died. It made her feel as if the cottage had shut its eyes.

Her mum got Alfie out of his car seat and carried him to the front door. Turning the key, she pushed the door open. Maia followed her inside. The cottage was dark and cold, and there were packing boxes in the hall.

For a moment, Maia pictured the cottage as it used to be – lights on, the smell of biscuits baking, Granny Anne standing in the kitchen making tea with her special red kettle that whistled when it boiled, the smile on her face as she saw Maia…

Maia backed out of the cottage. Being there made her feel too sad.

Her mum saw her face. "Are you OK?"

"Can I go for a walk?" asked Maia. "I'll just go to the waterfall."

"That's fine," her mum said, "but don't go any further than that. Have you got your phone with you?"

Maia nodded and fled.

Chapter Two

Maia hesitated at the side of the lane. If she carried on down it she would eventually reach the beach. Instead she crossed over it and headed on to an overgrown path that led into the woods opposite the cottage. Brambles caught at her legs, their branches heavy with ripe blackberries. Maia edged round them and pushed through the drooping cow parsley. She breathed in the earthy smell and started to feel calmer. Pulling her coat closer round her, she hurried on down the path until she emerged into a clearing. At one edge of it, a waterfall flowed down a set of mossy stone steps and then ran away in a gurgling stream.

Maia breathed out. The clearing was one of her favourite places in the world. She and Granny Anne always used to come here. In the spring they had watched the birds and counted the squirrels while the new leaves opened on the branches. Now the leaves were falling from the trees and the clearing was overgrown.

Maia wrapped her arms round herself and sat down on an old tree stump. It felt like everything was changing. *I don't like it*, she thought. *I don't want things to change.*

She swallowed as she remembered Granny Anne sitting beside her, pointing out things. "That's a blackbird … and can you see the little wren over there? Oh, and look, there's a unicorn in the trees, Maia!" When Maia had swung round, Granny Anne had laughed. "You missed it that time. But keep watching and one day you'll see it, too – or if not a unicorn, you'll see something else magical, I promise. You just need to believe."

And Maia did believe. She would never admit it to anyone at school apart from Sita and Lottie, but she did still believe in magic even though she was in Year Six. She squeezed her arms tighter round herself. *I do believe*, she thought to the Granny Anne in her head. *I always will.*

"Hello," said a voice. "Can you hear me?"

Maia's eyes flew open. She looked this way and that but there was no one about. She must have imagined the voice. But then her eyes caught sight of a movement in the trees behind her. A young fox with a rusty-red coat came creeping out. He had large pointed ears, a bright, intelligent gaze, a fluffy snow-white chest and a bushy tail that looked like the end of it had been dipped in white paint.

Maia hardly dared to breathe. He was beautiful.

The tip of the fox's tail started to wag as he edged closer to her. As he got nearer, Maia saw that his eyes were a deep indigo blue. That was weird. She thought foxes had brown or hazel eyes.

Her phone rang, shattering the peace, and the fox raced away. Maia cried out in frustration and pulled out her phone. Her mum's name appeared on the screen. She quickly answered the call. "Hi," she said, her eyes searching for the fox in the shadows of the trees.

"Hi, sweetie," her mum said. "Dad's here and we're ready to go now. Can you come back?"

"Um, yeah, sure," said Maia, still looking for the fox. He had gone. She sighed. "I'll come now."

She ended the call and, taking one last look, she left the clearing.

Her mum and dad were locking up the cottage when Maia got back.

"Hi, there," her dad called. "Ready to go home?"

Maia nodded, still thinking about the fox with the strange eyes. And what about the voice she had heard? She was sure someone had spoken to her in the clearing.

Her dad scooped up Alfie into his arms. "Come on then, young man. Into my car."

"Car!" said Alfie in delight, hitting Mr Greene on the head with the plastic car he was holding.

"Yes, car!" Mr Greene said ruefully, rubbing his head.

"I thought I would pop in to see Auntie Mabel on the way home while Dad and Alfie pick up Clio," Mrs Greene said to Maia. "Would you like to come with me?"

"OK," said Maia. She liked Auntie Mabel.

The old lady had been one of Granny Anne's closest friends.

They got into the car and drove up the lane to the main road. "Look, there's Ionie," said Mrs Greene, spotting Ionie in the garden of her house at the top of the lane. "Do you want to stop and say hi?"

Maia shook her head. "No, just keep going."

To her relief, her mum didn't insist.

Auntie Mabel lived in a row of cottages on the main road. She had grey hair and blue eyes that twinkled in her wrinkled face. When she opened the door to her cottage, the smell of baking wafted out.

"Well, this is a lovely surprise!" she said, smiling warmly as she saw Maia and her mum. "I wasn't expecting visitors today."

"We just thought we'd stop by and see how you were," said Mrs Greene.

"All the better for seeing both of you," said Auntie Mabel. "Come on in. I've got some biscuits here that need eating."

They followed her inside her cosy cottage. There were pictures of woodland animals on the walls and a collection of crystals and polished stones on the dresser in the kitchen. Auntie Mabel put the kettle on and soon they were all eating freshly baked shortbread and talking about the memorial service that had been held for Granny Anne two weeks before.

"The church was packed, wasn't it?" said Mrs Greene.

"Anne was very well loved," said Auntie Mabel. "All her life. Right from when we were children. She was always the popular one."

"Well, she did love helping people," said Mrs Greene. "And she got involved in so many things here in Westcombe – raising money for charities, making the village more eco-friendly, saving the wildflower meadows."

"She's certainly going to be missed," Auntie Mabel agreed. "Anyway, how are all of you?

How's school, Maia?"

"Oh, OK." Maia caught sight of a little oil painting of a fox stalking some rabbits and it made her think about the fox in the wood. "A really weird thing happened to me earlier," she said. She told them about the fox. "He came almost close enough for me to touch."

Her mum raised her eyebrows. "That's unusual. Foxes are shy creatures."

"Your granny used to have a knack with wild animals," said Auntie Mabel. "Maybe you take after her."

Maia liked that idea. "I hope I see him again," she said. "He had strange eyes – they were a really dark blue – like an indigo colour."

"That can't be right, Maia," her mum said. "Foxes don't have indigo eyes. It must have been a trick of the light."

Auntie Mabel gave Maia a thoughtful look. "Or maybe it was just a very unusual fox. I'd love to know if you see him again, Maia. He sounds fascinating."

Maia nodded, glad Auntie Mabel believed her at least. "I'll tell you if I see him."

As the conversation moved on, Maia tuned out of the adult talk and thought about the fox. Sita and Lottie were coming round in the morning, but maybe she could go to the clearing again in the afternoon. She could take some bits of ham in case he was there.

She pictured him eating from her hands, looking up at her with those strange eyes. They *had* been indigo. She was sure it hadn't just been a trick of the light.

Maybe he's a magic fox. No. That was silly, she told herself. But her heart beat just a little faster at the thought.

Chapter Three

The next morning, Maia went to the kitchen and got out everything she thought they might need to prepare for their cake sale – recipe books, baking trays and all the ingredients. The evening before, she'd told her mum and dad, and they thought it was a fantastic idea.

She had just finished getting ready when Clio came into the kitchen in her dressing gown. She looked round at all the baking equipment. "What are you doing?"

"Sita and Lottie are coming over for a

practice baking session."

"Oh, for the cake stall you were talking about yesterday. I'll make some brownies for you, if you like," Clio offered.

"Thanks." Maia smiled. She and Clio were very different – Clio loved make-up, fashion and gossiping about celebrities whereas Maia liked playing outside, baking and making things with her friends. Still, most of the time they got on just fine. Not like Lottie and her little sister, who argued constantly.

"What are you doing today?" Maia asked as Clio made herself some toast.

"Seeing Beth. We're going shopping." Her phone buzzed and she checked it. "OMG!" she said. "Did you know Maddie and Jay have split up?"

"Who?" said Maia.

Clio stared at her. "Seriously? Maddie and Jay? You know – the YouTubers?" Maia gave her a blank look. "How can you not know these things? Sometimes I can't believe we're sisters. I've got to phone Beth!" She hurried out of the kitchen.

Maia shook her head. She just didn't get her sister's fascination with celebrities.

At nine o'clock on the dot, Lottie's mum dropped her friends off.

"I'll see you at eleven fifteen," she said to Lottie. "Make sure you're ready for me and changed into your gymnastics kit."

"Yes, Mum," Lottie sighed. Her mum hurried back to the car, where Lottie's younger sister was waiting to be taken to her tennis lesson.

"You and your sister do so many things," said Maia as Lottie dumped her bag in the hall.

"Gymnastics, tennis, piano, swimming, maths

and French." Lottie ticked them off on her fingers. "Oh, and now Mum wants us to start trampolining lessons, too."

"We'll never see you!" said Sita.

"Sleepovers," Lottie said decisively. "Even my mum can't schedule activities in the middle of the night."

"Sleepovers sound good to me," said Maia. "How about having one here the night before the cake sale?"

The others nodded enthusiastically.

"So, what cakes are we going to bake?" Lottie said. "We need a plan!"

They sat down with the recipe books.

It didn't take Maia long to decide. "Chocolate fudge cupcakes for me!"

Lottie turned a few more pages. "I think I'll do lemon cupcakes."

"I'm not sure," said Sita.

Maia and Lottie started measuring out the ingredients they needed for the first batch of cupcakes while Sita kept looking.

"Watch out! Here comes the flour!" cried Maia, tipping the flour from the scales into the mixing bowl with a flourish. A cloud of flour flew up into the air.

"Maia!" exclaimed Lottie, pointing to the recipe book. "It says you're supposed to sieve the flour into the mixing bowl, not just tip it in."

"Too late!" Maia grinned, wiping flour from her nose.

"But we should do what the recipe says," protested Lottie.

"I don't mind sieving it," said Sita reaching for the mixing bowl and carefully tipping the flour back into the packet. She was always the peacekeeper. "You two get on with something else."

"OK. I'll prepare the cupcake cases on the baking trays," Maia said.

"So, have you decided what you want to bake, Sita?" Lottie asked as she started chopping butter into cubes.

"Not yet," Sita admitted. "I don't know whether I should do chocolate chip or carrot cupcakes."

"Chocolate chip," Maia decided for her.

"But…" began Sita.

"Nope, it's decided," said Maia firmly. She knew if she didn't choose for her, Sita would probably still be trying to make up her mind on the day of the cake sale!

They settled down happily to bake and soon three trays of cupcakes were ready to be cooked. While the cakes were in the oven they started clearing up, but when Sita flicked a dishcloth full of soap suds at Maia it quickly turned into a water and soap fight.

Then they had to clear up the water and soap suds before Maia's mum came in. At last everywhere was looking clean and tidy and the cakes were cooling on wire racks.

After Lottie was picked up by her mum, Sita and Maia began designing some posters to advertise their cake stall. When the cakes had cooled they iced the tops and decorated them with sprinkles.

"Mmm. Those cakes smell good," said Maia's mum, coming into the kitchen with Alfie on her hip.

"Want one!" Alfie exclaimed, wriggling and reaching out for the gooey cupcakes.

"Is he allowed one?" Sita asked Maia's mum.

"Well, I was about to make lunch but a little taste won't hurt," said Mrs Greene.

Maia and Sita cut up one of each type of cupcake for them to try.

"More!" said Alfie, banging the tray of his highchair.

"I feel the same way," said Mrs Greene. "But we'd better wait until after lunch. You've done a great job, girls. I bet you'll sell lots of these at the Harvest Show. Now, would you like to stay for lunch, Sita?"

"No, thank you. My mum is expecting me home," said Sita.

Maia and Sita packed two tins with cakes. Sita took one tin for her family and promised to drop off the other at Lottie's house. "I hope you see that fox again this afternoon," Sita said to Maia as she left. While they'd been making the posters, Maia had told her about her encounter with the fox and her plans to go back to the clearing that afternoon.

"I hope so, too," said Maia.

"Phone me if you do," said Sita.

"I will," Maia promised with a smile.

✦ ✦ ✦

After lunch, Mrs Greene drove to Granny Anne's to collect some more boxes. "I'm going to the clearing, Mum," Maia said as she got out of the car.

"OK. Don't be more than fifteen minutes though – I'm just planning on grabbing some things and going. You've got your phone, haven't you?" her mum said.

Maia nodded and then hurried across the lane and on to the overgrown path that led into the woods. *Oh, please be here!* she thought as she jumped over brambles and pushed aside the cow parsley. As she reached the clearing, a squirrel scampered down a tree trunk and a flock of sparrows chattered in the branches. She looked all around but there was no sign of the strange fox with the blue eyes. Disappointment washed over her. For some reason, she had felt sure he was going to be there. She sat down on a tree stump. Maybe if she waited for a while he'd come back…

She blinked. The fox was there – at the edge of the clearing. It was as though he had appeared out of thin air.

Maia started to reach for the plastic bag with the ham but he was already bounding over. He stopped and stared up at her. As Maia gazed into his dark blue eyes, she heard a voice say, "You came back."

Maia felt a rush of shock. The fox had just spoken to her, she was sure of it. But he couldn't have! Animals couldn't talk. She must be going mad…

The fox continued to stare intently at her. "You can hear me, can't you? Please say you can."

Maia swallowed. The fox's mouth wasn't moving but she could hear him in her head. It seemed impossible but she knew she could.

"You can … you can talk?" she whispered.

The fox gave an excited yip. "You *can* hear me!" he said. "As soon as I saw you yesterday, I was sure there was something special about you. I felt it with every hair of my body. You must believe in magic."

"I–I do," Maia stammered.

The fox put his paws on her knees and licked her nose. "I'm Bracken. What's your name?"

"Maia," she just about managed to say. It was like she was in some sort of strange dream.

Bracken bounded away and then crouched

down in a play bow, his bushy tail waving in the air. "Hunter said we'd know! I can feel you're the right person for me. Will you be my Star Friend, Maia?"

Maia didn't have a clue what he was talking about but this was amazing – awesome! Magic *was* real, just like Granny Anne had always said. "Yes! I'll be your Star Friend," she said. "But … what is a Star Friend?"

Bracken trotted over. "There's so much I've got to tell you. I come from a place called the Star World. Magic flows between our worlds and I've come here to find a Star Friend, someone I can teach how to use magic. Star Animals help their Star Friends to do good deeds and they stay friends together forever."

Maia's thoughts spun. "So if I'm your Star Friend, you'll be with me forever and I'll learn how to do magic?"

Bracken nodded, his eyes shining. "If you want to."

"Oh yes!" What would Sita and Lottie say when she told them? A thought struck her. "Bracken!" she exclaimed. "My best friends believe in magic. Could they be Star Friends, too?"

"Maybe," Bracken said, looking excited. "The other Star Animals haven't found Star Friends yet. But to be a Star Friend, you have to really believe in magic. Don't tell anyone about it until we know whether they can be Star Friends, too. The Star World has to stay completely secret. We think there might be other people – bad people – who are using magic to do evil. The less they know about us, the better."

Maia's mind raced. "OK. I won't tell anyone, I promise."

"Thank you!" Bracken bounded round her in a circle. "I'm so happy I found you, Maia. We're going to have so much fun together!"

He took a flying leap into her arms and

licked her nose.

Her heart swelled happily. This was incredible! "I'll ask if Sita and Lottie can come round first thing in the morning. If they can, I'll bring them here."

Bracken nuzzled her. "I'll make sure the other Star Animals are here then, too."

"I'd better go now," said Maia. The last thing she wanted to do was leave him, but she didn't want her mum coming to look for her. "Bye, Bracken, I'll see you tomorrow morning." Maia kissed him one last time on the nose, and then put him down and ran back to the cottage, her thoughts tumbling over and over in her head.

She couldn't believe what had just happened to her. It was magic – *real* magic! This had to be the best day of her life!

Chapter Four

"Mum! Mum!" Maia gasped, bursting into Granny Anne's cottage. Her mum was kneeling in the hall, putting some old diaries into a box. Maia skidded to a halt. "Please can Sita and Lottie come round tomorrow? I have to see them!"

Her mum smiled. "You can't be missing them that much. You only saw them this morning."

"I know, but this is important. I've … um … I've had an idea for a really good game in the clearing and I want to play it with them. We could cycle down here. You don't need to give us a lift."

"OK. That's fine by me, as long as their mums are happy, too." Mrs Greene dusted her hands down. "Auntie Mabel's here. She popped in to see if I needed a hand so we decided to do a bit more sorting out."

"Hello, Maia," said Auntie Mabel, appearing in the dining-room doorway. She looked at Mrs Greene. "The china in the dining room is all packed up. I'll just check the sideboard drawers to make sure they're empty. Do you want to help me, Maia?"

"OK," Maia said, following her back into the dining room. She felt like she was going to explode. If only she could tell someone what had just happened to her!

"I was thinking about you this morning, wondering if you'd see that unusual fox again – the one you were telling me about," said Auntie

Mabel, opening the top sideboard drawer and checking inside.

"I saw him just now," Maia burst out. She paced around the room, too excited to do something as boring as checking drawers.

"Really? And were his eyes blue?" Auntie Mabel asked curiously.

Maia hesitated, remembering her promise to Bracken. Maybe she shouldn't say anything more. "I didn't get close enough to see," she lied.

"Maybe they are … and maybe he's a magic fox." Auntie Mabel winked at her over her shoulder.

Maia stared. What did that wink mean? Could Auntie Mabel possibly know about Star Animals?

Just then Maia's mum came in with two cups of tea and a glass of juice on a tray. "Time for a break, I think. Thanks for helping, Mabel."

"It's my pleasure, dear," said Auntie Mabel,

checking the final drawer in the sideboard. "All these drawers are empty now. Oh, wait a minute. What's this?" She pulled something out from the very back of the drawer. It was a slim, round silver make-up compact with a pink enameled lid.

"That's pretty," said Mrs Greene, taking it and opening it up. There was a mirror on one side and a pressed circle of make-up powder on the other.

"It is, isn't it?" said Auntie Mabel, taking a sip of her tea.

"Would you like it?" Mrs Greene offered the compact to her. "It's not been used."

"Oh no, I've no use for make-up on my old face," Auntie Mabel said with a chuckle. "Why doesn't Maia have it?"

"OK." Maia put down her glass and took the compact. She had no use for the face powder either, but the case was pretty and she liked the fact that it had belonged to Granny Anne. She slipped it into her pocket. "Can I ring Sita and Lottie now and see if they're free to come tomorrow?"

"Sure," her mum said.

Maia went out to the front of the cottage where the phone signal was better. Lottie was at swimming so she left a message. Sita answered though.

"So we're to bring our bikes?" Sita said, when Maia explained what she wanted.

"Yes. We're going to cycle to the woods near Granny Anne's," said Maia.

"Where you saw that fox? Did you see him again today?" Sita asked.

"You'll find out tomorrow," Maia said, hoping she was right. She ended the call and hugged the phone to her chest.

Oh, please let Lottie and Sita be Star Friends, too! she thought.

Maia was still buzzing with excitement when she got home. She danced around the kitchen, where Clio was sitting at the table reading a magazine.

"What's up with you?" she said in surprise.

"Nothing. I'm just happy," said Maia.

She remembered the compact in her pocket and pulled it out, turning it over to look at it.

"That's pretty. Where did you get it?" Clio asked.

Maia passed the mirror compact to Clio so she could take a look. "It was in one of the drawers at Granny Anne's house. Auntie Mabel found it."

Clio opened it and looked at the mirror.

"You can have it if you want," said Maia with a rush of generosity. "I don't need it."

"Thanks!" Clio smiled. Her phone buzzed. She checked the screen and gasped. "No way!

Guess what's just happened to Beth!"

"What?" said Maia.

"She's been asked to model for a magazine! Oh, wow, I am *soooo* jealous!" Despite her words, Clio didn't sound it, she just sounded delighted for her friend. She hurried out of the kitchen. "Beth!" Maia heard her squeal as she headed up the stairs. "That's awesome. What happened?"

Maia shook her head. If Clio thought *that* was awesome, what would she think about what had happened to *her* that day?

She wondered if there were other Star Friends nearby and what their Star Animals were. Suddenly she remembered what Auntie Mabel had said about Bracken being a magic fox and a thought struck her. Maybe *Auntie Mabel* was a Star Friend! And what about Granny Anne? Could she have been a Star Friend, too? She couldn't wait to see Bracken again – there were so many questions to ask!

"This path is really overgrown," said Sita the next morning as she edged round a giant fern on the way to the clearing. The sky above was blue with wispy white clouds trailing across it. They'd cycled to Granny Anne's cottage together and left their bikes in the garden.

Lottie jumped over a mossy rock. "Why is it so important that we come here today, Maia? What have you got planned?"

"It's a surprise," Maia said. Butterflies fluttered in her tummy. What was going to happen when they all reached the clearing? She remembered Bracken's words from the day before. *To be a Star Friend, you have to really believe in magic.* Lottie and Sita always said they believed in magic, but did they mean it? What if they couldn't hear the Star Animals speak? She swallowed as an even worse thought hit her – what if only *one* of them could?

Lottie looked at her warily. "You know I don't like surprises."

"This will be a good one," Maia said, crossing her fingers.

When they reached the end of the path, Lottie and Sita looked around the clearing.

"Um…" said Lottie, looking confused. "What's the surprise then?"

Maia chewed her lip. "Well…" She wasn't quite sure what she'd imagined would happen when they got there – maybe that Bracken and the other Star Animals would all be waiting. *I should have made a plan,* she realized.

Lottie and Sita were both looking at her expectantly.

"The um … the surprise will be along in a moment." Maia glanced round. *"Bracken! Bracken!"* she called in her head. *"I'm here! Where are—"*

Sita made a sharp intake of breath. "Look! It's a deer! Oh, isn't she beautiful!" A young deer with a coat gleaming like a conker stepped out of the trees. She stopped and stared at them with huge eyes, her delicate ears twitching. A red squirrel scampered down a tree and ran up beside the deer. It sat down on its haunches and looked curiously between the girls, and then an otter poked its head out of the river.

"There are so many animals here!" said Lottie as a sparrowhawk flew down from the trees and landed on a rock, a badger shuffled from underneath a bramble bush and a dormouse ran out. Finally a sleek wildcat with slanted eyes slid out from the shadows.

All of the animals stared at the three girls.

"Oh … my… *Wow!*" breathed Lottie, staring around. "What's happening?"

"Is this the surprise, Maia?" whispered Sita.

Maia nodded.

"But how did you know these animals would be here?" Lottie said in amazement.

Bracken came trotting out of the trees. Maia felt a rush of happiness as her eyes met his. He touched her hand with his nose. She heard him say, "Hello, Maia. Are these your friends?"

Lottie and Sita both gave strangled squeaks.

"That fox! He just *spoke*!" said Lottie, pointing at Bracken.

Maia looked from her to Sita. "Did you hear him too, Sita?" she asked.

Sita nodded wordlessly.

Delight rushed through Maia. "If they can hear you, that means they can be Star Friends, too, doesn't it, Bracken?"

Bracken spun round in delight. "Yes!" He turned and looked at all the watching animals – the otter, the squirrel, the deer, the hawk, the badger, the dormouse and the wildcat. "The question is – whose Star Friend are they going to be?"

CHAPTER FIVE

"What … what's going on, Maia?" Lottie said uncertainly.

"It's magic," Maia said in a rush as she looked around the clearing at the beautiful animals, all with sparkling indigo eyes. "These animals come from another world – the Star World. They're each looking for someone to be their Star Friend. They'll teach that person how to do magic to make good things happen." She turned to Bracken in excitement. "That's right, isn't it?"

He nodded. "Maia's my Star Friend," he told Lottie and Sita. "She said she thought you might both be Star Friends, too – and she was right!"

"I'd love to be a Star Friend!" Sita gasped, her eyes as wide as saucers.

"Where is this Star World? Can we go to it?" asked Lottie eagerly.

"No, I'm afraid not," said Bracken. "Only Star Animals can travel between the worlds."

"But you're saying we can learn to do magic here?" said Sita.

Bracken nodded.

"What sort of magic?" Lottie asked.

"That will depend on your own natural abilities," said Bracken. "But first you need to find out which of us is your Star Animal."

"Do we choose or do they?" said Lottie, looking around at all the animals.

"It can be either way," said Bracken. "But you both have to feel it in your hearts."

To Maia's surprise, Sita suddenly started walking towards the deer. "Hello," she whispered, holding out her hand. "I don't know how I know this but I think I'm meant to be your Star Friend."

The deer sniffed her hand. She wasn't tall — her head was only just higher than Sita's hip and her eyes were huge, fringed with curling lashes.

"I think you're right," she said. "I feel like I know you already. My name's Willow."

"I'm Sita." Sita put her hand on Willow's neck and Willow sighed happily.

Maia glanced at Lottie. Lottie was looking at the rest of the animals — the badger, the dormouse, the wildcat, the sparrowhawk, the otter and the squirrel. "You're all so beautiful," she whispered.

The squirrel scampered across the clearing towards her. "But I'm the one you should choose! I just know I am!" He stood up on his hind legs and stared at her with his small bright eyes. "I'm Juniper. What's your name?"

"Lottie," Lottie said.

Juniper leaped on to the tree trunk beside her, then on to a branch and hung upside down.

Lottie giggled. "I can do that, too." She did a handstand and looked back at him.

Juniper made a chattering sound as if he was laughing. "You're supposed to be my Star Friend!"

As Lottie turned the right way, Juniper leaped from the branch and landed on her shoulder.

A smile spread across Lottie's face as she

touched his soft red fur. "Yes, you're right," she declared.

Bracken yipped.

"The rest of us must keep looking for our Star Friends," said the badger rather sadly. "Come. We should move on."

The animals headed into the trees. The otter paused and looked back at the wildcat, who was still standing there. "Sorrel, are you coming?"

The cat yawned, showing sharp white teeth. "Maybe I will, maybe I won't. I'll please myself."

Bracken made a grumbling noise in his throat. "As always."

Maia glanced at him and saw he was looking at the cat with dislike.

The cat – Sorrel – stood up, shook her paws daintily and then stalked into the trees in the opposite direction to the other animals.

"She seems kind of prickly," Maia whispered to Bracken.

The fox nodded. "She is. I'm glad neither of your friends chose her to be their Star Animal."

Maia turned to look at Lottie and Sita. Sita was stroking Willow and they were speaking softly to each other. Lottie was sitting cross-legged, giggling as Juniper ran up one arm, behind her head and down the other.

Maia felt a burst of happiness. They were all Star Friends! "Can we start learning to do magic now?" she asked.

Bracken leaped into her arms. "You can, but first I think we need to tell your friends more about where we've come from."

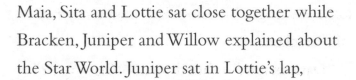

Maia, Sita and Lottie sat close together while Bracken, Juniper and Willow explained about the Star World. Juniper sat in Lottie's lap,

Willow lay beside Sita, her slender legs folded underneath her, and Maia sat with her arm round Bracken, stroking his thick fur.

"So, what's the Star World like?" asked Lottie.

"Beautiful," said Juniper. "Everything shines and sparkles."

"It must have been really hard to leave," said Sita.

"It was," said Willow. "But we wanted to come here to help. Humans need people in their communities who know how to use magic to do good, people who can solve problems, stop arguments, look after the environment, and heal things and people."

"And we were told we were particularly needed here, in this area," said Bracken.

"Why?" said Lottie.

"The older animals in the Star World think someone might be using dark magic nearby," said Bracken.

"Dark magic," echoed Sita. "What's that?"

Willow's ears flickered anxiously. "Dark magic is the opposite of Star Magic. It comes from the ground and it is magic that can be used to hurt people and make them unhappy. If someone is using dark magic near here, they must be stopped."

"Will stopping them be dangerous?" Lottie breathed.

Juniper nodded. "Yes. But we'll have each other." He stroked her hair with his little paws.

Maia felt a mixture of excitement and nerves bubbling up inside her. Stopping someone doing dark magic sounded scary but thrilling, too. "When can we start learning to do magic ourselves?"

Bracken jumped up. "Right now!"

"The sooner the better!" said Juniper, scampering after Bracken.

"Oh, yes!" said Willow, her dark eyes shining as she stood up. "We need to find out what your magic abilities are. Everyone is different."

"What do we have to do first?" Maia asked eagerly.

"Star Magic is all around you. It flows in a current, like a stream, from the Star World to the human world. You just need to open yourself up to it," said Bracken.

"How?" asked Lottie.

"Have any of you ever had times when you've felt completely lost in the moment?" Willow said.

"I have," said Sita. "Sometimes when I lie on the heather up on the clifftops with the sun on my face, everything else in the world just seems to fade away."

"That's happened to me, too," said Maia, remembering times when she'd been lying on the beach or sitting in the clearing, watching the waterfall.

"And me – when I've been floating in the sea," said Lottie. "Or sometimes when I'm playing a piece of music I really love, I feel like I get lost in it."

Juniper waved his tail. "That's exactly the feeling you need to find now – exist in the moment, open your hearts and the Star Magic will flood in."

"Don't try and *make* it happen, just *let* it happen," advised Willow. "If you think about it too much, I don't think it'll work."

Maia looked around at the others. "Come on! Let's try!"

Chapter Six

Maia, Lottie and Sita shut their eyes.

Forget everything, Maia told herself. She tried to push all her thoughts out of her head but for some reason she found herself picturing what she might have for lunch – sandwiches maybe or pizza… She shook her head. No. She needed to concentrate. If she didn't, the others would start doing magic and she wouldn't be able to. That would be awful. She pictured Sita and Lottie doing amazing things while she just watched…

"Maia." She heard Bracken's voice. "Don't think about anything else. Just focus on being here, in this moment."

Maia took a deep breath and focused on the clearing. She could hear birds in the trees, the splash of water. She could smell fallen leaves and moss. She didn't think about anything else. Her body started to tingle slightly. She caught her breath. Was this it? Was she about to do magic? It would be so cool. What would she be able to do? The tingling feeling faded.

"Maia, stop thinking about it. Just let it happen," Bracken said.

Maia heard Sita give a gasp. "Oh, wow!"

Maia desperately wanted to open her eyes. What was Sita doing? Had she discovered what magic she could do?

Bracken stepped on to her knees. "Stroke me, Maia. Don't think about anyone else. You need to lose yourself in the moment so the magic can come in."

Maia ran her hands down Bracken's fluffy coat. She concentrated on the feeling of his soft fur as she stroked his body over and over, breathing in his warm scent. The tingling feeling started again but this time she didn't stop and think about it, she just relaxed. The tingling spread from her toes to her head. She felt like every bit of her was waking up, opening like a flower in the sun. She felt linked to the whole world, joyful, alive…

"You've connected to the magic," Bracken said. "Open your eyes."

Maia opened her eyes. Everything looked sharper, as though she could see each blade of grass, every vein on every leaf, every hair on Bracken's russet-red body. She slowly looked around. Lottie was still sitting on the ground, her face screwed up in concentration. Juniper was sitting on her shoulder.

"You're trying too hard, just relax," Maia heard him say.

Bracken bounded in front of her. "What do you feel?"

"Like I can see everything really clearly," breathed Maia.

"That could mean your magic abilities are to do with sight," said Bracken. "I think I know how to find out for sure." He bounded to the stream. "Take a rock out of the water."

As Maia looked into the stream, she gasped. She could see through the swirling eddies to the pebbles and rocks below, the little fish slipping through the weeds, the water beetles spinning round. "It's like I'm looking through a magnifying glass."

"With the power of sight you'll be able to do far more than just see everything around you really clearly," said Bracken. "Look into the surface of a wet rock and say the name of someone you know."

Maia took a rock out of the water, wondering what was going to happen. The surface shone like a mirror. "Mum," she whispered. She almost dropped the rock in surprise as a faint picture appeared in the wet surface. She could see a fuzzy image of her mum in the kitchen at Granny Anne's, cleaning the cupboards.

"What do you see?" Bracken said.

"My mum. Look."

"I can't see it," he told her, shaking his head. "It's your magic that lets you see the image. As you practise more, you'll be able to use shiny surfaces to see what's happening elsewhere really clearly, you'll be able to hear what's being said and look at the details of a scene. You'll also be able to see the past and glimpses of the future, and you might even learn to see into people's minds."

"Oh, wow!" said Maia, her thoughts racing. She glanced around and saw Sita touching a broken stem of cow parsley. As she ran her fingers along it, the stem strengthened and repaired until it was tall and strong again. "Look at that!" she said.

"Sita's abilities must be to do with healing," said Bracken.

Sita came over with Willow beside her. Her eyes were shining. "I feel amazing!" She took Maia's hands in hers and Maia immediately felt soothed, as if someone had wrapped a cosy blanket round her shoulders. "Willow thinks I'm going to learn how to comfort people and heal them," said Sita. "Can you do that, too?"

"No, my magic's different – it's to do with seeing things," said Maia.

Lottie cartwheeled over the clearing towards them, jumping to her feet after the fifth cartwheel. "Every bit of me is bursting with energy. I want to run and jump and climb!"

"Then do it," urged Juniper, scampering up a tree. "Come on!"

Lottie shot up the tree trunk after him, as agile as a squirrel herself. They climbed high into the tree in just a few seconds. Straddling a branch, she wrapped her legs around it and hung down. "Look at me!" she cried, waving at them.

"Be careful!" exclaimed
Sita.

"Don't worry," Willow
said. "Her magical
abilities must be to do
with agility."

"When she's using her
magic, she'll be able to do
things a normal human couldn't,"
added Bracken.

As if to prove his point, Lottie pulled
herself upwards, climbed on to the branch
and then jumped down to the ground
easily, turning a forward roll as she landed
and springing lightly to her feet.

"This is awesome!" she said, beaming.

"Now you've connected with Star
Magic once, you'll find it much easier
next time," Juniper said. "If you practise,

you'll soon be able to use your magical abilities in the blink of an eye. But now you should release the magic. It will tire you out if you use it for too long at first."

"How do we release it?" Sita asked.

"Imagine you're closing a door on it in your mind," said Bracken.

Shutting her eyes, Maia did as he said. The feeling of energy faded and when she blinked her eyes open, the world was back to normal again. She felt slightly dizzy. She swayed and looked at the others – they looked slightly wobbly, too.

"We should practise every day," said Lottie.

Juniper jumped on to Lottie's shoulders. "You should all start using your abilities to help people. Even if it's just with small things. When you use magic to do good, the magic current will be strengthened and your magic abilities will grow."

"What about dark magic?" said Maia,

looking at Bracken. "What happens when people use that?"

Bracken's ears flattened. "Dark magic comes from the ground. Bad people can use it to conjure Shades – evil spirits who exist in the shadows. Once a Shade has been conjured, it can be released into the world to bring misery and unhappiness. It can also be trapped inside an object like a necklace, book or toy that the person using the dark magic will give to someone they want to hurt or harm in some way."

"How can a Shade harm someone?" said Lottie.

Juniper swung on to Lottie's other shoulder. "Some Shades whisper to people, encouraging their worst feelings of jealousy, anger and greed, twisting their minds. Other Shades bring nightmares to life or trap people using magic or cause accidents to happen. There are many different types. If we find a Shade trapped in an object, we must release it and send it back to the shadows."

"But only a Spirit Speaker can do that," Bracken put in.

"What's a Spirit Speaker?" asked Sita curiously.

"Some Star Friends are called Spirit Speakers because they have the magic ability to command spirits. But none of you seem to have that ability," Bracken answered. "If we find an object with a Shade trapped in it, we'll just have to hide it where no one else will ever find it."

"And stop the person who conjured the Shade in the first place," added Juniper.

Willow shivered. "We'll have to be careful. If someone is using dark magic, it could be very dangerous."

"I don't care," said Maia determinedly. "I'm not scared."

"Me neither," said Lottie.

"So, how do we find out if someone is using dark magic?" Sita asked.

"We need to look out for strange things happening, people acting in unusual ways or people being exceptionally unhappy, miserable, hurtful or scared," Bracken said.

"I think the older Star Animals are right and someone is using dark magic," said Willow. "As soon as we got here I could smell it in the air – a hint of sourness that wafts in and out. It makes the hairs on my back prickle."

"What about you, Bracken?" asked Maia. "Can you smell dark magic, too?"

He shook his head. "Not all Star Animals can. It's a bit like different humans having different magical abilities. Willow is sensitive to dark magic and can smell it. I can't."

"Sorrel – the wildcat – is even more sensitive than I am," said Willow. "I am able to smell a hint of dark magic in the air but she is able to follow the scent of it."

"Will she help us?" asked Lottie eagerly.

"No," said Willow. "She'll be travelling on now to find her own Star Friend."

"We don't need her anyway," declared Bracken. "We'll be fine on our own."

Maia nodded. "We'd better keep our eyes and ears open for anything weird going on," she said, looking at Lottie and Sita, who both nodded.

"And, in the meantime, we should keep learning to use our magic," said Lottie.

"This is all so amazing!" said Sita, stroking Willow. "I can hardly believe it."

Maia crouched down and hugged Bracken. Sita was right. It *was* amazing! In twenty-four hours everything had changed. She didn't know where it was all going to lead but one thing was for sure, their lives were never going to be the same again!

CHAPTER SEVEN

When Maia got home, she went straight up to her room. She wanted some time on her own to think about everything that had happened. As she reached the top of the stairs, Clio came out of her bedroom.

"Do you think I'm pretty?" Clio asked.

Maia was taken aback. "What?"

"Do you think I'm pretty?" Clio demanded.

"Um … yes," said Maia.

"Not as beautiful as Beth though?" Clio persisted.

"Well … Beth is really, really pretty," said Maia, thinking of Clio's friend with her waist-length dark hair and olive skin. "Like stunningly, model-looking pretty."

Clio frowned and pulled the compact out of her pocket to look at her reflection. "It's not fair," she grumbled. "Why should Beth be so perfect? Why should she be the one who gets to be a model?"

Maia edged past her. Clio was so busy looking in the mirror that she didn't seem to notice.

"OK, and today's prize for the weirdest sister goes to Clio Greene," Maia muttered as she reached her room.

Shutting the door after her, she sank down

on her bed. Alone at last.

Maia remembered what Bracken had told her as she had left the clearing. He had said that now she was his Star Friend, he would always appear if she called his name. She decided to try it. "Bracken?" she whispered.

There was a shimmer of starlight and then Bracken appeared, his ears pricked, his tail waving.

"Hello!" he said, leaping on to the bed.

She hugged him, burying her face in his soft fur.

As he nuzzled her neck, she felt a wave of happiness sweep over her.

"So, did you like doing magic today?" he asked.

"Definitely!" she said. "It's brilliant that Lottie and Sita are Star Friends, too." She stroked his back. "Are there any others around here? Or is it just us?"

"Just you," said Bracken.

"Are you sure?" Maia remembered what she had been thinking about the night before. "It's just that there's this old lady I know – Auntie Mabel – she was friends with my granny who died last month. I was wondering if she might be a Star Friend and … well … if my granny might have been one. Granny Anne definitely believed in magic and she was always helping people."

Bracken looked puzzled. "There are definitely no other Star Animals anywhere near here – only the ones I travelled with. We would have sensed any others when we arrived. The old lady you're friends with can't be a Star Friend."

"Oh," said Maia, disappointed.

"Maybe she's the kind of person who could have been a Star Friend but never met a Star Animal," Bracken suggested. "That sometimes happens. However, your granny might have been a Star Friend. When she died her Star Animal would have returned to the Star World." He nuzzled her. "I can't say if she was or not but I'm sure that if your granny was a Star Friend she'd be really pleased to know you are one, too, Maia."

She hugged him tightly and an image of Granny Anne's smiling face filled her mind.

Bracken licked her hands and Maia felt a new determination steal over her.

I'll do my best to be a good Star Friend, she told

Granny Anne in her head. *I promise I'll make you proud.*

✦ ✦ ✦

It was very hard waiting for afternoon to come the next day. Maia longed to go to the clearing and start practising magic again, but Lottie was busy with activities all morning and Sita was out with her family. The day seemed to crawl by but finally it was three o'clock, and Lottie and Sita arrived at Maia's house on their bikes. They set off to the clearing straight away.

As they turned on to the lane that led to Granny Anne's, they passed Ionie playing in her garden with her two rabbits. She looked up but they didn't stop. Maia felt a pang of guilt as they cycled past. But she couldn't stop and say hi, she and the others wouldn't be able to do magic if Ionie joined them.

Cycling on down the lane, they left their bikes in Granny Anne's garden and pushed their way down the overgrown path. As soon as they ran into the clearing, Bracken, Willow and Juniper each appeared out of thin air. Juniper scampered up Lottie's arm and jumped on to her head, making her giggle. Willow danced round Sita and then butted her gently with her head and Bracken bounced around doing play bows and barking. They seemed as happy as the girls to all be together.

"Let's do more magic," Maia suggested, shooting a look at Lottie and Sita. They both nodded eagerly and sat down on the grass with their animals beside them. Maia breathed in and out, opening her mind, letting all her thoughts fade away. She felt the tingling start and magic flowed into her. Opening her eyes, she saw everything with super sharpness again.

Sita and Lottie were already on their feet.

Lottie turned two handsprings effortlessly. "I feel brilliant!"

Sita smiled happily. "It's the best feeling.

I just want to go and help people."

"Me, too. I wish…" Maia broke off. She felt as if her eyes were being drawn towards a patch of brambles at the edge of the clearing. She frowned. Why did she feel she needed to look at that spot?

"What is it, Maia?" Sita asked.

"Shh." Maia held up a hand. She could tell that something was wrong, something needed help. She looked into the bushes and concentrated hard. Normally she'd only be able to see a cluster of bramble bushes but now she could see *through* the branches. There was an animal there – a young squirrel caught in the thorns. It was struggling but it couldn't get free.

"Over there," said Maia, pointing. "There's a squirrel who needs help."

They all followed her to the patch of thick brambles. Now they were closer they could see the branches moving. Not caring about the thorns that caught at her skin, Maia pulled the branches apart. "Look!" The little grey squirrel froze for a moment and then struggled harder, getting even more tangled up.

"You can help it," said Bracken. "Work together."

"Sita," said Willow. "Use your magic to calm it first."

Crouching down, Sita reached into the branches. As she murmured to the squirrel, it stopped struggling. She touched it and all the little animal's tension and fear seemed to drain away. It stared at her with trusting dark eyes. She gently untangled the brambles from its fur and lifted the squirrel out.

"You poor thing," she soothed, stroking its coat and letting it nestle against her.

"That could be its drey up there," said Maia, spotting a nest made of leaves and twigs, high up in a fork in one of the branches.

Juniper scampered up the tree and inspected the drey. "Yes, this is where it lives," he called. "Lottie, can you bring it up? Then it can recover in safety."

Lottie took the squirrel from Sita. Maia wondered if it would start to panic again but it seemed to accept them as friends now. Lottie tucked it into her coat and started to climb the tree. As she did so, Maia blinked. Her eyes felt weird. It was as if she could see where Lottie would climb a second before she did it.

"Bracken! I can see what she's going to do before she does it," she whispered.

"It must be part of your magical ability," Bracken said. "You can probably choose to use it or not. Try and control it with your mind."

I want to see normally! thought Maia. It was too weird seeing a second in advance.

To her relief, her eyes returned to seeing things in normal time, although she could still feel Star Magic tingling through her.

Lottie reached the fork in the tree and placed the squirrel inside its nest. Juniper chattered at it and it chattered back. Then Lottie and Juniper climbed down the tree. Lottie jumped the last few metres. "It's safe up there," she said.

They all exchanged happy smiles.

"That was fun," said Sita. "I want to help something else." She glanced at Maia's hands. "Maybe I can heal your hands?"

Maia had been so busy thinking about the squirrel that she hadn't noticed her hands hurting. Looking down, she saw they were covered in scratches. She held them out.

Sita touched them. Maia felt a soothing warmth and the scratches stopped bleeding but they didn't disappear completely.

Sita looked disappointed. "I can't seem to help more than that."

"Don't worry," said Willow. "I'm sure if

you keep using your magic you'll be able to soon." Suddenly she tensed, her large ears swivelling. "Someone's coming!"

The Star Animals vanished just as Ionie appeared in the clearing.

"Hi," said Sita, smiling at her.

"What are *you* doing here?" Lottie said.

Ionie raised her eyebrows. "I live near here. What's your excuse? I've seen you coming here every day." She gave them a curious look. "Why?"

"It's none of your business," said Lottie.

"We just like it here," said Sita.

"We're going now anyway," said Maia.

"You don't have to," Ionie said quickly. "You can stay if you want."

"Um … actually we'd better go," said Maia, feeling awkward. "Mum will be wondering where we are."

"OK. Whatever," Ionie said, shrugging and scuffing her foot on the ground. "Bye."

Maia, Lottie and Sita headed for the path. As they were about to leave the clearing, Maia glanced back. Ionie was watching them go with an almost wistful expression on her face. Maia suddenly felt bad and took a step back towards her, but Ionie turned away quickly and hurried into the trees.

Chapter Eight

"Morning," Maia's mum and dad said when Maia went downstairs for breakfast the next day. She'd slept well with Bracken curled up at her feet. He'd promised he would vanish if anyone came in, but he hadn't had to and it had been lovely to wake up and cuddle him.

"Hi." Maia poured herself some cereal. She waved at Alfie who was in his highchair. He pulled his dirty bib up over his face, peeking out from behind it.

"Alfie, don't do that – you'll get porridge in

your hair," her dad said, pulling the bib down so he could spoon some porridge into Alfie's mouth. Alfie took a mouthful but then blew a raspberry so that it all spattered over Mr Greene. "Alfie!" he groaned.

Maia handed him a cloth. "Now you've got porridge in *your* hair!" Mealtimes were always messy when Alfie was involved. Keeping a safe distance from the highchair, she sat down with her own cereal.

"What time are Lottie and Sita coming over?" her mum asked.

"At nine thirty," said Maia. "We're going to finish the posters for our cake sale and put them up around the village so everyone knows about it." *And after that we'll cycle to the woods and practise doing magic again*, she added to herself, her heart racing at the thought.

"OK, well I'm dropping Clio at Beth's for an hour or so while I take Alfie on a play date, but Dad will be here if you need him. If you go out, tell him where you're going." Her mum went to the door. "Clio! You need to have some breakfast before I drop you at Beth's."

A few minutes later, Clio came downstairs in her pyjamas and dressing gown. Her hair was dishevelled and there were faint grey shadows under her eyes.

"Ce-o!" Alfie crowed. It was his way of saying her name.

Clio ignored him. Maia frowned in surprise. Usually Clio made a big fuss of their little brother. But now she just pulled out a chair and slumped into it.

"Toast?" her mum said, handing Clio a plate. "You'd better get a move on — we've got to leave in fifteen minutes."

"I can't be ready by then!" Clio pulled the compact out of her dressing-gown pocket and checked her reflection. "I look awful. I need at least half an hour."

"You're only going to Beth's house. Give your hair a quick brush and you'll be fine," Mrs Greene said.

"But I have to do my make-up! Beth always looks great." Clio looked at herself from different angles in the compact and examined a small spot on her chin. "It's not fair," she muttered. "Beth never gets spots. Why does she get to be so perfect?"

Maia looked at her in surprise. She was used to Clio laughing about how annoying it was to have a beautiful best friend like Beth, but today she sounded genuinely resentful.

"Clio! Put that mirror away and eat your

breakfast!" said Mrs Greene, scooping the compact out of Clio's hands and putting it on the table. Clio grabbed it and stuffed it in her pocket. She sat munching her toast, not saying another word.

"Teenagers!" Maia saw her dad mouth silently at her mum.

Maia finished her cereal. "I'm going to get dressed."

"Will it take you half an hour to get ready, Maia?" her dad asked with a grin as he cleared away the remains of Alfie's porridge.

She grinned back at him. "Oh, at least."

Knowing she was being teased, Clio scowled at them both and stomped back to her room.

Mr Greene shook his head pityingly. "It's hard being fifteen," he said.

"I heard that!" Clio shouted down the stairs.

As soon as Sita and Lottie arrived, they raced up to Maia's room. They were going to finish the posters with the door shut so Bracken, Juniper and Willow could appear.

"I used my magic last night," Sita said excitedly, as Maia closed the door and the three Star Animals appeared.

"What did you do?" Maia asked as Bracken bounded round her legs.

"Rohan was crying and Mum couldn't settle him." Rohan was Sita's baby brother. "When Mum went out of the room, I used my magic. I sensed he had a tummy ache. I put my hands on his tummy and felt the pain fade away. And then he stopped crying and went to sleep. Mum was really pleased."

"That's so awesome!" said Maia.

"It felt brilliant," said Sita, her eyes shining.

Willow nuzzled her hands. "You're going to be an amazing healer, Sita. I know you are."

"I did something, too," said Lottie, stroking

Juniper. "The little boy next door had been playing with his Frisbee. It got stuck on the garage roof and I heard him crying. When he went inside for his tea, I checked there was no one watching and used my magic to climb up a drainpipe and get it. He was really surprised when he came out after tea and found it on the ground. His mum said the wind must have blown it down." She grinned. "But it wasn't the wind, it was me!"

"Cool!" said Maia, wishing she had a story to tell, too. "I didn't do anything magical. Bracken and I just talked. I'll have to try and find something to do today." She grinned at the others. "I can't have you both doing magic and me not."

"Are we going to go to the clearing?" Juniper asked. "I like it there. It's a good place for playing and practising magic."

"It is," agreed Willow. "The air smells sweet because there's lots of Star Magic there."

"We can go in a bit – but first we've got to finish making posters," Lottie said. "The cake sale is on Saturday – in four days' time. We need to get some posters up so that people know about our stall and what we're raising money for. That way, people will buy lots of cakes."

Maia got out the posters. "We'd better get started then."

When the posters were finished, they set off around the village on their bikes to put them up. Their first stop was the village hall where, to their surprise, they found Ionie standing by the noticeboard.

"Hi," said Sita as they got off their bikes.

Ionie smiled back. "Hi."

"Are you putting up a notice, too?" Maia asked her.

"Yes, I'm organizing a decorate-a-biscuit stall in aid of endangered animals at the Harvest Show," said Ionie. "You should come along." She looked at them. They were all staring at her. "What?" she said.

"But … but we're doing that!" Maia burst out. "Well, we're organizing a cake stall and that's pretty much the same thing."

"You stole our idea!" Lottie said.

Ionie's eyebrows shot up. "I so didn't!"

"You must have done!" exclaimed Lottie. "You must have been spying on us!"

"Seriously? You're not that interesting, and I've got better things to do with my time than spy on you!" Ionie snapped.

"It's obvious there's just been a mix-up," said Sita. "It's funny in a way – I mean, both you and Maia having the same idea." She looked around hopefully but none of the others smiled back at her.

"Why don't we all do a stall together?" she hurried on.

"Ionie could have one end of the table for decorating her biscuits and we could sell cakes at the other end. After all, we're raising money for the same cause, so it's a bit crazy to have two stalls. We'll probably raise more if we join forces."

Lottie glanced at Maia.

"All right," Maia muttered. "You can share with us, Ionie."

"Thanks." Ionie rolled her eyes. "But no."

"What?" Maia frowned.

Ionie gave her a haughty look. "I know you all might find this impossible to believe, but I don't want to have a stall with you. I'd rather do my own thing."

"Ionie, that's silly…" Sita began.

Ionie shrugged. "Well, it's what I'm going to do." She stalked off.

"She's *so* annoying!" Lottie burst out.

Sita sighed. "To be fair, we didn't make it sound like we really wanted her to share with us. I don't blame her for saying no."

Maia felt a flicker of guilt.

Lottie put her arm through Maia's. "Come on, let's put up the rest of the posters and then go to the clearing. I want to do some more magic!"

A smile caught at Maia's lips. "Me, too," she said.

Chapter Nine

"That was even easier than yesterday!" Maia said, opening her eyes and looking around at the clearing as she let Star Magic flow into her.

Bracken wagged his tail. "I told you it would get easier every time."

Sita came over with Willow. "My magic feels much stronger today. Can I have another try at healing those scratches on your hands?"

Maia held out her hands. Sita touched the scratches and shut her eyes, breathing deeply. Maia felt warmth flood over her skin and the scratches tingled. She gasped as they started to shrink and fade, then vanish completely.

"Sita! Look!"

"I did it!" Sita said in delight.

Maia turned to Bracken, even more eager to do something herself. "What should I try?"

"Why don't you work on using your sight to find out what's happening elsewhere?" he said. "If you practise, you should be able to hear what's being said. You might be able to find out if anyone needs help. You just need something that reflects light to look into."

"I should have kept that compact I gave Clio," Maia said. "I could have used the mirror in that."

She took another rock out of the river and sat down on a tree stump, holding it in her hands.

"Think about something or someone you really want to see," said Bracken.

Maia thought about Clio. She let the magic

flow from her into the rock she was holding. An image appeared in the shining surface. It was a fuzzy picture of Clio in her bedroom.

"Can you see anything?" Bracken asked.

Maia nodded. "Yes, I can see Clio. But it's not very clear."

"Try to relax and just let the magic flow," suggested Bracken.

Maia breathed slowly in and out. "It's working," she said as the image came into focus. Clio was sitting at her desk, the compact in her hand. She seemed to be talking to someone but there was no one there. Maia frowned. Maybe her phone was on speaker?

Maia heard a faint buzz and then, little by little, she began to make out what Clio was saying.

"You're right, it's really not fair," Clio was muttering angrily. "Why should the good things always happen to her? What about me?" Maia watched as her sister brought the compact closer to her face. "You understand, don't you?" she said to the mirror.

Maia stared. Clio was talking to her reflection! That was seriously odd. She blinked and let the vision fade.

"What did you see?" Bracken asked.

"Clio was being really weird," said Maia.

Bracken pricked his ears hopefully. "If she's unhappy in some way, maybe you can use magic to help her."

"I'm not sure how," said Maia. "It sounds like she's mad at her best friend Beth for being so pretty. Maybe I should try and see if I can find someone else who has a problem."

Bracken nodded and Maia used the rock to see her mum. An image appeared showing her searching for her purse with Maia's dad.

"Where did you have it last?" her dad was asking.

"At the petrol station," her mum said. "But I rang them and they said they haven't found it. If I don't find it soon, I'll have to cancel all my bank cards."

Maia had an idea. "Mum's purse," she said to the rock.

The image rippled and changed to show her mum's purse. It had been pushed under the bookcase in the lounge – probably by Alfie. Maia pulled out her phone and texted her mum.

Hi Mum. Just remembered – I meant to tell you, I saw Alfie playing with your purse in the lounge, near the bookcase. Mxx

She said her mum's name and watched in the rock as her mum checked the text, then hurried to the bookcase. Her face lit up as she pulled the purse out from underneath it. "It's here!" she called to Maia's dad. She took out her phone.

A few seconds later, Maia's phone pinged with a text.

Thank you! Just found it! Phew! X

Maia smiled. OK, it had only been a small thing but it had definitely been a good deed. She let the vision fade.

"So? What happened?" Bracken said.

When Maia told him, he jumped round her, his tail waving.

Maia grinned. "I know what magic I want to practise next," she said. "That weird thing I did the other day where I can see where people are going to move before they actually do."

"Try with me!" said Bracken. "Use your magic to see which way I'm going to go and try and tag me!"

He stood in front of her, poised and ready.

Maia concentrated
on letting the
strange feeling
creep into
her eyes. She
nodded at him.
"Left!" she
shouted, a fraction
of a second before
he actually moved. She
sprang to the left at the same
time, reaching out with her hand and
touching his soft fur.

Bracken rolled on to his tummy and jumped
to his feet. "That was good! Try again."

This time she tagged him as he sprang to
the right.

"What are you doing?" Lottie asked.

Maia explained.

"Let's all play!" said Lottie.

Soon Maia was chasing everyone. It was

much more fun being
It in a game of tag
if you could see
where people
were going to
go! She tagged
Sita, Bracken,
Willow and
Juniper easily. The
only person who
managed to get away
from her was Lottie and
that was only because she could
move so fast. Maia chased her around
the clearing, changing direction a split second
before Lottie did each time but never quite
managing to tag her with her outstretched
hand. Lottie was faster than a cheetah!

In the end they stopped and fell on the
grass together.

"That was fun!" said Lottie, her eyes shining.

Maia laughed and stretched out her arms above her head.

"Well, I'm definitely never playing tag with either of you again!" Sita said with a grin.

"I guess we'd better go home," said Maia, sitting up reluctantly.

"When we meet up next we should try and think up a plan to find out if dark magic is being used nearby," said Sita, glancing at Willow. "Willow says she feels sure that something is going on."

Willow pawed at the grass uneasily. "I keep getting a scent of dark magic but I can't work out exactly where it's coming from."

Bracken pricked his ears. "Maybe we can all figure it out over the next few days."

Sita, Maia and Lottie got back to Maia's house just as Lottie's mum arrived.

"Have you had fun?" Lottie's mum asked,

helping her put the bike in the boot of the car.

"Yep!" said Lottie, winking at the others. "Lots and lots!"

Sita said goodbye and cycled off. Maia waved to Lottie and then went inside. Clio was in the hall.

Maia looked at her closely, remembering how weirdly she'd been behaving when she'd watched her in the rock. "Hi," she said.

"Hi," Clio muttered.

"Are you OK?" Maia said.

"Yes. Well, I mean obviously I'm not as pretty as Beth in your eyes and obviously I shouldn't be a model like Beth should," she said. "But apart from that I'm just fine." She stalked through to the lounge.

Maia stared after her and then went into the kitchen. Her mum was helping Alfie paint a picture.

"Mum," Maia said. "Do you think Clio's acting a bit weird?"

"In what way?' her mum said.

"I don't know," said Maia. "It's just she keeps saying stuff about not being as pretty as Beth."

"Oh, that's just Clio being fifteen," her mum said, turning her attention back to Alfie. "Paint the paper, Alfie, not your hands. "At that age you have days when life doesn't seem fair and it feels like no one understands you. Don't worry about it. She'll get over it in a day or two."

Maia bit her lip.

Her mum glanced up, saw her worried face and gave her a quick smile. "It's sweet of you to be concerned but really, she's fine, Maia."

"OK." Maia sighed, hoping her mum was right.

CHAPTER TEN

Over the next few days, Clio didn't become her normal teasing, gossiping, cheerful self again. If anything, she became even more grumpy and lost in her own thoughts. If she did speak to Maia, it was only to snap at her.

Most of the time Maia was too busy practising magic or talking to Bracken to think about it much. But on Thursday evening, Maia knocked on Clio's bedroom door to make sure she'd remembered her offer to make chocolate brownies for the cake sale on Saturday.

No one answered but the door was ajar so Maia pushed it open and looked inside. Clio wasn't there. Maia's gaze was caught by a glint of light. The compact was on the desk, its lid open. As she looked at it, Maia felt a sudden strange urge to pick it up.

She walked into the room and reached for it.

"What are you doing?" Clio's voice snapped. Maia swung round. Clio was standing in the doorway. She strode over and grabbed the compact. "That's mine!"

Maia recoiled in shock as Clio stepped forwards threateningly. "Get out of my room!" she yelled.

"Sorry!" Maia ran out.

The door slammed shut after her.

Maia turned and stared at the door, her heart pounding. OK, Clio didn't like her going into her room but she'd never screamed at her like that before. Something very, very weird was going on. This wasn't Clio just being fifteen and moody.

She hurried back to her room. "Bracken!" she whispered.

Bracken instantly appeared and bounded up to her. "Are we going to do something? Shall we try practising your magic again?" He stopped, putting his head on one side. "Are you all right, Maia? You seem upset."

"Mmm," she said distractedly.

He stood on his back legs and put his paws on her knees. "What's the matter? You can tell me."

She hugged him. "I'm worried about Clio. She's acting so strangely. I just went to her room and she was really odd."

"Why don't you use your magic to see what she's doing now?" Bracken said.

Maia went over to her bedroom mirror. Taking a deep breath she opened herself to the current of magic. "Clio," she whispered. The mirror shimmered and then an image of Clio appeared in the glass. She was sitting on her bed, talking to something in her hand. At first Maia thought it was her phone but then, as the vision got clearer, she realized that it was the compact again.

"I hate her," Clio was muttering to the compact. "You're right, I should do something about it. She deserves it."

A chill ran down Maia's spine. "She's talking to herself in the mirror again and saying really weird stuff," she said.

Bracken flattened his ears. "In a mirror? Oh no, no, no. Maia, this isn't good. Which mirror?"

Maia frowned. Why did that matter? "It's the make-up compact that used to be Granny Anne's. Mum said I could have it but I gave it to Clio a few days ago."

"About the time when she started behaving strangely?" Bracken asked. "Maia, we've been looking for evidence of dark magic – well, that mirror could have a Shade trapped inside it. Mirror Shades can work all sorts of evil. They manipulate anyone who looks into the mirror. They pretend to be that person's friend but then they start twisting their minds, making them jealous and angry."

Maia's heart felt like it was in her throat. "Then what happens?"

"If the Shade isn't stopped, the person can end up doing dreadful things."

Maia frowned. "But Bracken, the compact was Granny Anne's. How can it have something evil in it? Granny Anne would never have something evil in the house."

"If she was a Star Friend, she might well have tried to hide it to make sure that no one else would use it," Bracken said.

Maia swallowed. It made horrible sense.

"We've got to get the mirror away from Clio. But it won't be easy," she said, thinking about how angry Clio had been when she had found Maia near the compact in her room. "What should we do?"

"I think we should contact the others and come up with a plan together," said Bracken.

Maia nodded. "It's too late for them to come over now but they're coming round tomorrow and sleeping over, so we can work out what to do then." She sank down on her bed. Bracken jumped up beside her and she pulled him on to her lap. "Oh, Bracken, Clio is going to be OK, isn't she?"

"I hope so," he said. "I really do."

Maia's dreams that night were full of dark shadowy figures hiding in mirrors and mocking her. She woke up feeling sick with worry. Was there really a Shade in Clio's compact? Was that why her sister had been acting so strange and scary? Even cuddling Bracken didn't help her feel better. She just wanted to rush into her sister's room and grab the compact, but even she could see that wasn't a good idea.

As soon as the others arrived, she took them upstairs. Bracken, Juniper and Willow appeared almost instantly.

"What's the matter?' said Sita, seeing Maia's face.

Maia told everyone about the compact.

Willow sniffed at the air and her ears flickered anxiously. "Bracken's right. I can smell the sour scent of dark magic here."

"What are we going to do?" Juniper ran along Maia's bed and jumped on to the back of her chair. "If it is a Shade, we should send it back to the shadows. But because none of you are a Spirit Speaker, we can't do that."

"We need another plan then," said Lottie.

"The next best thing is to steal the compact and put it where no one will ever find it," said Juniper.

"Like Granny Anne tried to," said Maia.

"When Clio leaves her room, I could sneak in and get it," said Lottie. "I'll use my magic to move really fast."

But Clio's door stayed firmly shut. In the end they went downstairs to start making the cakes.

✻ ✦ ✻

"Lunchtime!' Mrs Greene called up to Clio
when the cakes were cooling on wire racks.

"She'll have to come out now," Maia
whispered to the others.

Clio came downstairs but Maia saw the
shape of the compact in the pocket of her
jeans. Now what were they going to do?

Clio hardly said a word at lunch. When Maia
asked her when she was going to make the
chocolate brownies, she shrugged and didn't
give an answer. As soon as she could, she went
back upstairs and shut her door. Maia thought
over various possibilities while she, Lottie and
Sita iced and decorated the cupcakes. How
could they get hold of the compact? How
could they get Clio out of her room?

At six o'clock, her mum served lasagne
and salad and Clio finally emerged from her
room again.

"Aren't you and Dad having supper with us?" Maia said when her mum didn't sit down.

"No, we're going to pop next door for an hour or so. We'll take Alfie with us. Clio, you're in charge of everyone else while we're out."

Clio hunched over her plate, pushing the food around with her fork.

"OK, Clio?" Mrs Greene said.

"Mmm," Clio muttered.

Mrs Greene smiled at the rest of them. "If you need us, just give us a ring."

Once Mr and Mrs Greene had left with Alfie, Clio took the compact out of her pocket and began to open it up. Maia, Lottie and Sita exchanged glances.

"That's nice. Can I see it?" Lottie asked, reaching out.

"No!" Clio snapped, pulling the compact away and shutting it quickly.

They carried on eating in an uncomfortable

silence. They had just finished when the doorbell rang.

Maia jumped up, glad of an excuse to escape the tension at the dinner table. "I'll get it."

She went to the door. Beth was standing on the doorstep. "Hi, is Clio there?" she asked.

"Yeah," said Maia. "Come in."

Beth followed her inside. Clio was in the kitchen doorway. She scowled when she saw Beth. "What do you want?"

Beth blinked in surprise. "I … I just thought I'd come over to see you. You've been really weird the last few days. Are you OK?"

Clio glared at her. "Like you'd care."

Confusion crossed Beth's face. "What do you mean?"

"Oh, don't act like you don't know. All you care about is yourself." Clio's face creased in an ugly sneer. "I'm Beth, the model. I'm Beth and I'm so beautiful. No one else matters."

"What are you talking about?" Beth asked.

"You think you're so perfect, don't you?"
Clio said angrily. "Well, no one else thinks so
and no one likes you and soon – very soon –
you'll be sorry!"

"Clio!" Maia burst out, seeing the shocked
look on Beth's face.

"I'm not listening to this," Beth said, her
eyes filling with tears. "I don't know what's up
with you."

Beth turned and ran out of the house, and Clio marched upstairs.

"Beth! Wait!" called Maia, but Beth didn't stop.

Lottie and Sita hurried out of the kitchen. They had obviously heard every word of the argument.

"What do we do now?" said Lottie.

"We have to get that compact," said Maia.

"Maybe I could get it when she goes to sleep," said Lottie.

"We can't wait until then." Maia thought for a moment and then nodded. "OK, how about this for a plan…"

CHAPTER ELEVEN

Ten minutes later, Sita stood outside Clio's bedroom door with a mug of hot chocolate decorated with whipped cream and tiny marshmallows. Maia was in her bedroom, using her magic to watch in her bedroom mirror and Lottie was in the garden below with Juniper.

Bracken nuzzled Maia's hands. She stroked his head gratefully as she heard Sita knock on Clio's door. Would the plan work? The first part of it depended on Sita's ability to get Clio out of her room.

"Clio, it's Sita," Sita called softly. "I've brought you a hot chocolate."

The door opened. Clio gave Sita a suspicious look. "Where's Maia?"

"With Lottie," Sita said. "Are you OK?"

She handed Clio the hot chocolate. As Clio took it, Sita's hand closed gently on her arm. "You seemed really upset earlier," she said, her voice sympathetic.

Clio's frown began to fade as Sita touched her.

"I have been feeling odd," she admitted slowly. "I don't know what's been the matter with me this week."

"Why don't you come downstairs with me and have a talk about it?" said Sita gently. "Simi, my big sister, says I'm a good listener. I'd like to listen to you."

Maia held her breath, hoping Sita's persuasive, calming magic would work and that Clio would go with her.

To her relief, Clio nodded. "OK, but don't go in my room." She shut the door firmly. "I'll hear if anyone opens the door," she warned.

"No one will open your door," Sita promised. She led Clio downstairs, shooting a quick look over her shoulder and winking.

Maia ran to her window. "Lottie!" she hissed into the dusky garden. The next part of the plan involved Lottie getting the compact – without using the bedroom door, just in case Clio decided to check.

"On to it!" Lottie whispered back. Maia watched as she grabbed hold of the Virginia creeper that covered the house and pulled herself easily up the wall. Juniper scampered beside her and stopped by the window. It was just slightly ajar. Lottie pulled it open and then Juniper leaped inside. Lottie followed him.

"Time to go, Bracken," Maia said. She and Bracken ran as quietly as they could along the landing and down the stairs. She paused on the bottom step. She could hear Sita talking soothingly to Clio in the lounge. "It must be awful to feel like that. You look so tired. Why don't you have a rest?"

Clio yawned. "Now you say it, I do feel tired."

"I'll shut the curtains," said Sita. "And then you can have a little sleep. I'll make sure everything is OK."

Maia slipped past the lounge door and ran into the kitchen. The French windows were open and she could see Lottie outside.

"Got it!" Lottie hissed, holding up the compact. Juniper was on her shoulder.

Maia took the compact from Lottie. Her heart was pounding. "Should I open it?" She looked at Bracken.

"We do need to find out if there's a Shade in there," he said. "But be careful, Maia."

"Really, really careful," said Sita anxiously as she came out through the French windows. "Clio's asleep now."

Maia opened the compact and looked into the mirror. As she did so, she caught sight of a shadowy grey shape flickering deep in the glass. The image grew clearer, becoming the reflection of a handsome boy with tousled blond hair and dark eyes.

"*What have we here?*" a voice said in her head. "*Not my Clio but someone else. A Star Friend for me to have fun with!*"

Maia felt anger surge through her. "Clio's not your Clio and yes, I'm a Star Friend, but you're not going to do anything with me."

"*Really?*" The Shade's voice was like golden syrup, smooth and tempting. His eyes looked deep into hers, kind and understanding. "*Don't you want to be special, Maia? Being the middle child must be hard. Your parents adore little Alfie and his funny ways and Clio's the eldest, the firstborn. She'll always be the one they love most. That leaves you… Well, where does it leave you?*"

His hypnotic voice wove its way into Maia's mind. He was right. She was just the middle one. Her parents did love Alfie and Clio more…

"Maia!" Bracken said. "Don't listen to the Shade. Use your magic to fight it."

With an effort, Maia connected to the

magic current. As magic flowed into her she looked at the Shade – properly looked at it. The handsome face and sympathetic brown eyes melted away under her gaze, becoming a grey skull with glittering red eyes. The spell it was casting was broken. "No!" she cried. Repulsed, she threw the compact down.

The mirror smashed as it hit the ground. Juniper chattered and Willow bleated in alarm. Grey smoke started to seep out through the cracks in the broken glass.

"What's happening?" cried Lottie.

Bracken jumped in front of Maia as the smoke swirled together and formed a very tall thin figure with grey skin, a skull-like face and ragged clothes. The figure's slanted eyes glowed red in his bony face. Seeing the horror on the girls' faces, he laughed and stepped towards them.

"Finally, I am free!" He cracked his long bony fingers then he pointed at Maia.

"Thank you, my dear. I never imagined you'd give me my freedom. You really have a lot to learn." He rubbed his hands together. "Now I can roam where I like, inhabit any mirror I like, cause whatever mischief I like."

"No!" she said bravely. "I won't let you."

The Shade laughed. "And how do you plan on stopping me? I see three Star Friends here but not one of you is a Spirit Speaker." He spread his fingers. Sharp nails popped out like knives.

"What shall we do?" Sita gasped.

The Shade stepped towards them.

Bracken growled. "Stay back!" Darting forwards, he grabbed the Shade's leg with his teeth.

At the same moment, Willow charged and butted the Shade. Juniper leaped on his head.

"No!" the Shade hissed, swiping at them with his long nails.

He caught Bracken's side, making the fox yelp.

"Bracken!" cried Maia. She threw herself at the Shade. He stood his ground and, as she hit his chest, he threw her backwards as easily as if she weighed no more than a piece of paper. She landed on her back on the ground with a thump. The next moment the Shade was looming over her, laughing and showing off his teeth. "You think *you* can attack *me*?"

"Maia! Use your sight!" Bracken said.

She saw the Shade swipe down with his left

hand a second before he actually made the
move. She rolled to the right and jumped to
her feet just as Sita threw a plant pot at him.

"Get off her!" Sita shouted. It hit his side,
making him stagger.

Lottie grabbed a second plant pot from
the patio and charged at the Shade, using her
super-speed to dodge his hands with ease. She
hit him on the head. "Got you!" she gasped as
he fell to the ground.

The Shade slowly sat up. Bracken growled
warningly at him, Juniper chattered and Willow
lowered her head as if she was about to charge
again.

Maia heard his silky smooth voice. "*Well,
aren't you all very clever?*" he said. "*Really very
clever indeed… But who is the most clever? Who
is going to be the* best *Star Friend? Who will be
able to do the* most *magic? Don't try and tell me
you haven't thought about that! Will it be you,
Sita? Or you, Maia? Or you, Lottie? Don't you*

*all secretly wish you could be the best? One of you
will be more powerful than all the others. I can see
that. But who will it be?*" His voice weaved its
way around their thoughts. Maia found she
couldn't stop listening to it. She stared at him,
aware the others were staring, too.

"You should all just sit down and let me slip
away," said the Shade. "Then you can work out
between you who is the strongest, while I
find more mirrors to inhabit, more people
to enchant."

No, Maia wanted to say, but she couldn't get
the word out. Instead she found herself starting
to nod in agreement, caught in the Shade's
persuasive spell.

"Oh, I don't think so!" a familiar voice
rang out.

Maia blinked. The spell the Shade had
been casting faded in an instant. She swung
round and saw Ionie standing just inside the
garden gate.

"Ionie!" she gasped in astonishment.

Ionie put her hands on her hips and gave the Shade a level stare. "Your freedom is over, Shade." She held up her phone. "Smile!"

The Shade's face pulled into a grimace as the camera on her phone flashed. With a scream he dissolved into smoke and was sucked into the screen of the phone.

"Got him!" Ionie said triumphantly.

Maia, Sita and Lottie stared at her open-mouthed.

"Ionie?" Maia stammered. "What's going on?"

Ionie raised her eyebrows. "Honestly, Maia, I'd have thought even you could work this out. I'm a Star Friend, too, of course."

A wildcat with cool green eyes, a stripey tabby coat and large, pointed ears stalked out of the shadows. "And I'm her Star Animal," she said.

Chapter Twelve

For once Maia was lost for words. She glanced at Bracken. He looked as shocked as she felt.

Sorrel, the wildcat, looked around. "Well, this is fun," she said, her indigo eyes sparkling with amusement.

"How … how long have you been a Star Friend?" Sita stammered to Ionie.

"Since Monday," said Ionie. "Just after I saw all of you in the clearing, Sorrel spoke to me."

Bracken turned on Sorrel. "I thought you'd left."

Sorrel gave him a scornful look. "I'm a cat. We don't follow the pack. My instincts told me I should stick around." She purred and rubbed her body against Ionie's legs. "And I'm very glad I did."

Ionie touched her head. "So am I," she murmured, smiling.

"Ionie's exceptionally talented at magic," Sorrel announced smugly. "She's a Spirit Speaker."

"That explains why she managed to get the Shade to look at the camera so easily," said Bracken.

"A piece of quick-thinking," said Sorrel approvingly. "Did I mention, she's very clever, too?"

Maia could see why Ionie and Sorrel

had bonded! Still, though they were both annoying, Maia couldn't deny that Ionie had helped save the day. She shuffled her feet awkwardly. "Well … um … thanks for trapping the Shade," she said.

"Yes, thank you," said Sita. "I don't know what we'd have done if you hadn't been here."

Lottie nodded.

Ionie shrugged. "It's OK. I'm glad I could help."

Sita kneeled down by Bracken. His side was bleeding. "Here, let me heal you." She touched her hands to the wound and it closed up.

"Thank you," he said, licking her gratefully.

"What will you do with the Shade now you've trapped it, Ionie?" said Maia.

"You won't be able to use your phone while it's in there," said Bracken.

Ionie clicked on the photo and the girls saw the Shade moving angrily inside the screen.

"Careful!" Juniper burst out.

"I will not be kept in here!" the Shade ranted. "I will not! I—"

"Spirit, return to the shadows," Ionie said coolly. "I command it." She pressed DELETE.

For a moment the girls saw the Shade's face screw up in horror and then the photo vanished.

Ionie looked up and gave a grin. "Sorted," she said.

Sorrel weaved around her legs. "Oh, clever girl. Best of all possible Star Friends."

Lottie pulled a face at Maia. "Should I be sick now?" she muttered.

"Ionie," Sita said. "It's great you were able

to help … but why were you even here? Did you know about the Shade?"

Ionie shook her head. "Not for definite. Sorrel sensed something was wrong – she could smell it in the air – but she wasn't sure exactly what was happening."

Sorrel flicked her tail. "Cats are *far* more sensitive than other Star Animals," she said, giving the other three animals a superior look.

"I actually came round to talk about tomorrow," Ionie said. "I've been thinking about the Harvest Show. You're right, Sita – raising as much money as we can is the most important thing, so I wanted to say I'd share a table with you. When I got here we heard noises and came into the garden."

"Luckily for all of you," said Sorrel tartly. "You weren't handling the Shade very well on your own."

"We were fighting it off," said Bracken defensively.

"Star Friends are meant to trap Shades, not fight them," Sorrel said. "Or had you forgotten that? But I know it's hard without a Spirit Speaker. Luckily you have Ionie and me to help you now."

Maia exchanged looks with Lottie and Sita. She was relieved Ionie had been there to help them but she wasn't sure how she felt about Ionie and Sorrel hanging out with them regularly and helping them. Meeting her friends' eyes, she could tell they felt the same.

"I'd better get home. We'll see you in the morning," Ionie said. "Come on, Sorrel."

"Bye," said Sita.

"Yeah, bye," muttered both Maia and Lottie.

Ionie put her hand on Sorrel's head and the two of them seemed to vanish into thin air.

"Stealth," said Juniper, flicking his tail. "Ionie must have that magical ability as well as being able to command spirits."

"Great," said Maia, shaking her head. "So, she's doubly talented."

"Which will make her doubly unbearable!" said Lottie. "I don't want to have to work with them."

"It might not be that bad," said Sita hopefully.

"Someone's coming," Willow said, her ears swivelling towards the house.

The animals vanished just as Clio appeared.

She stood there groggily, swaying slightly. "I feel really strange," she said. "I've just woken up on the sofa but I feel like I've been asleep all day. Did I have an argument with Beth?"

"Yes," Maia said. "You weren't very nice to her."

Clio bit her lip. "I don't really remember it…" She shook her head. "I feel really dizzy and shaky."

Sita went over and put her hand on Clio's arm. "You've probably got a virus," she said soothingly. "That must have been why you were acting so strangely. I'm sure if you tell Beth that, she'll understand."

Clio nodded. "I'll phone her straight away and say how sorry I am."

"Yes, do that," said Sita.

Maia found herself nodding along with Clio. As Sita was growing stronger, it seemed like she wasn't just able to comfort and heal people, but she was able to persuade them to do things as well.

A puzzled look crossed Clio's face and she patted her jeans' pockets. "Has anyone seen my compact?"

Maia bit her lip. "I'm … um … sorry.
I borrowed it and I … well … I broke it."
She picked up the compact from the grass
and held it out. Clio looked at the cracked
mirror for a moment and then shrugged.

"OK, well, no big deal. It can go in the bin."

"She doesn't remember anything about the
Shade," hissed Lottie as Clio went back inside
and the animals all reappeared.

Juniper flicked his tail. "No, now the Shade
has been sent back to the Shadows, she won't
remember a thing."

Maia yawned and looked up, suddenly
realizing that night had fallen and stars
were twinkling in the dark sky. "It's been an
incredible day," she said.

"A bit too incredible for me," said Sita.
"How about we all go and have a hot
chocolate?"

"Good plan. We can eat some of our
midnight feast, too," said Lottie. "I know it's

only about seven o'clock but I think I need to do something normal for a while."

"Normal sounds good," said Sita.

They headed inside. Maia hesitated, looking at the compact in her hand. Now it was no longer inhabited by a Shade, it was just an ordinary silver and pink compact with a shiny lid and a broken mirror. So much had happened since Auntie Mabel had found it at Granny Anne's. It was so strange to think that Granny Anne had probably been a Star Friend, too – strange but comforting. *I wonder what's going to happen to us all next?* she thought.

The surface of the case started to shimmer. Maia caught her breath as she saw an image appear in it. It was a picture of herself, Lottie, Sita and Ionie at the cake sale. She was seeing the future! There were lots of people around their stall, the money pot was filling up with coins, and Clio and Beth were helping them, their argument apparently forgotten. That was good. The image changed. Maia saw herself talking to Lottie, Sita and Ionie in the clearing, their faces anxious. The images flashed by – a cave with a circle of candles, a girl holding her ankle and crying, a dark corridor with something moving in the shadows, a burning shed and then Maia herself with magic surging strongly through her, her hands raised. The images went faster and faster.

Maia. Bracken's voice broke into her thoughts.

She blinked and the pictures vanished. She took a shaky breath and slipped the compact into her pocket.

Bracken jumped into her arms. "What just happened?" he said softly.

"I think I saw into the future," she told him.

"What did you see?" he asked.

"Lots of things." She hugged him, thinking back over the images. "There's so much we're going to do."

Bracken nuzzled her neck. "I know. This is just the beginning, Maia. Someone must have put the Shade in that mirror. We need to find out who it is and stop them before they do anything else. We also have to figure out how to work with Ionie and Sorrel."

"I'm so glad I've got you," Maia said, kissing his head.

"You have," he replied, snuggling closer into her arms. "For always. Whatever's waiting."

Maia felt a warm glow tingle through her. As long as she had Bracken, nothing else mattered.

Just then, Lottie popped her head out of the French windows. "Are you two going to stay out there all night?"

"We're coming!" said Maia as the fox jumped down from her arms. With Bracken trotting at her heels, she headed inside to join her friends.

About the Author

Linda Chapman is the best-selling author of over 200 books. The biggest compliment Linda can have is for a child to tell her they became a reader after reading one of her books. Linda lives in a cottage with a tower in Leicestershire with her husband, three children, three dogs and three ponies. When she's not writing, Linda likes to ride, read and visit schools and libraries to talk to people about writing.

www.lindachapmanauthor.co.uk

About the Illustrator

Lucy Fleming has been an avid doodler and bookworm since early childhood. Drawing always seemed like so much fun but she never dreamed it could be a full-time job! She lives and works in a small town in England with her partner and a little black cat. When not at her desk she likes nothing more than to be outdoors in the sunshine with a hot cup of tea.

www.lucyflemingillustrations.com